Using th

When going through this book
with your child, you can either read through
the story first, talking about it
and discussing the pictures,
or start with the sounds pages
at the beginning.

If you start at the front of the book,
read the words and point to the pictures.
Emphasise the **sound** of the letter.

Encourage your child to think
of the other words beginning with
and including the same sound.
The story gives you the opportunity
to point out these sounds.

After the story, slowly go through the
sounds pages at the end.

Always praise and encourage
as you go along. Keep your
reading sessions short and stop
if your child loses interest.

Throughout the series, the order in which the sounds
are introduced has been carefully planned to
help the important link between reading and writing.
This link has proved to be a powerful boost to
the development of both skills.

SOUNDS FEATURED IN THIS BOOK

t i l f tr th ing
ie ll fl ff fr

The sounds introduced are repeated
and given emphasis in the practice books,
where the link between reading and writing is at the
root of the activities and games.

Ladybird books are widely available, but in case of
difficulty may be ordered by post or telephone from:

Ladybird Books – Cash Sales Department
Littlegate Road Paignton Devon TQ3 3BE
Telephone 0803 554761

A catalogue record for this book is available
from the British Library

Published by Ladybird Books Ltd Loughborough Leicestershire UK
Ladybird Books Inc Auburn Maine 04210 USA

Text copyright © Jill Corby 1993
© LADYBIRD BOOKS LTD 1993

Say the Sounds

Frog and
the lollipops

by JILL CORBY

illustrated by PETER WILKS

Tt

tiger

toy

let

but

tower

4

t

tortoise

tail

tell

went

tent

Ii

Say the sound.

Imp

if

in

it

hid

dish

wish

into

fish

i

ice cream

nice

like

fine

mine

bike

Ll

lollipop

ladder

log

leg

lion

leaf

l

ladybird

line

looks

lets

lamp

like

Ff

Say the sound.

fish

fat

fall

fun

fire

finger

f

face

first

fast

for

fence

Ben sees a troll. Jenny sees an imp.

The troll does not like
the imp and the imp
does not like the troll.

The imp is not nice to
the troll.

The troll is not nice to the imp.

The frog likes imps and trolls.

"One for you, Troll.
One for you, Imp.
One for you, Ben
and one for you, Jenny."

The troll does not like
the red lollipop.

The imp does not like
the green lollipop.

Now the imp has the red and the green lollipops.

Now the troll has the red and the green lollipops.

Now the frog has the green and the red lollipops.

The troll is sad.
The imp is sad.

They are sad.

The imp can not see the
green lollipop.
The troll can not see the
red lollipop.

They are sad.

Where are they?

Can you see the red and
the green lollipops?

Jenny and Ben and the frog have lollipops.

The troll and the imp are sad.

"Please can I have the red lollipop?" says the troll.

"Please can I have the green lollipop?" says the imp.

"You must be good, Imp.
You must be good, Troll,"
says the frog.

The imp and the troll must be good.

The frog says to the troll, "Please be nice to Imp."

The frog says to Imp, "Please be nice to Troll."

The troll must like the imp and the imp must like the troll.
They must be good.

"Yes, yes, yes!" they say.

"Here are the lollipops,"
says the frog.

"I have the red lollipop,"
says the troll.
"I have the green lollipop,"
says the imp.

tr

troll

tractor

train

treasure

tree

th and th

Can you hear the difference?

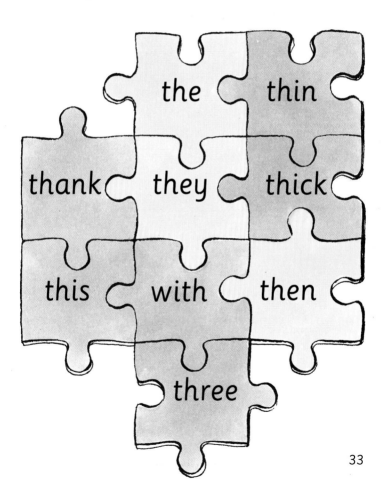

the

thin

thank

they

thick

this

with

then

three

ing

riding

talking

walking

singing

making

reading

Say the sounds.

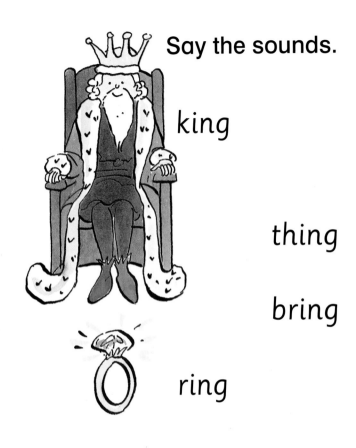

king

thing

bring

ring

ie   tie   lie

ll

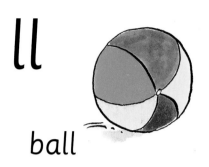

ball

well

fell

tell

hill

will

kill

mill

fill

Say the sound.

ll

yellow

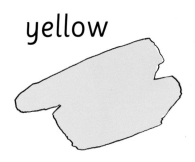

bellow

hello

willow

pillow

fl

Say the sounds.

flag

fly

flame

float

flip

flower

ff

quiff

puff

muff

huff

off

toffees

fr

freeze

frighten

frog

frost

fry

fruit

40

t i l f

Match the sound to the picture.

tr ll fl fr

Match the sound
to the picture.

New words used in the story

Words introduced 26

Learn to read with Ladybird

Read with me

A scheme of 16 graded books which uses a look-say approach to introduce beginner readers to the first 300 most frequently used words in the English language (Key Words). Children learn whole words and, with practice and repetition, build up a reading vocabulary.

Support material: Pre-reader, Practice and Play Books, Book and Cassette Packs, Picture Dictionary, Picture Word Cards

Say the Sounds

A phonically based, graded reading scheme of 8 titles. It teaches children the sounds of individual letters and letter combinations, enabling them to feel confident in approaching Key Words.

Support material:
Practice Books, Double Cassette Pack, Flash Cards

Read it yourself

A graded series of 24 books to help children to learn new words in the context of a familiar story. These readers follow on from the pre-reading series, **Read together**, and can be used in conjunction with any Ladybird reading scheme.